Wild Girl & Gran

NAN GREGORY • PAINTINGS BY RON LIGHTBURN

Red Deer Press

I am a princess in the castle keep.

I am a pirate on the high seas.

I am a cowboy on the lone prairie.

I am a wild girl alone in my stouthearted tree.

Up I climb. Look south, the flat sea sparks in the distance. Look west, the wind flaps Canada at the flagpole. Look over, my house through the trees.

When strangers invade, I curl up, still as an acorn. They pass under, watching where their feet go. No one sees me. No one.

The very afternoon my gran moves in with us, here she comes, jigging down the trail. Her cheeks are bright red add-ons. Her lips are dandy pink. Yarn loops higgledy-piggledy out of her shopping bag. I pull my feet up tight. I am an acorn. Gran will never see.

Below me on the trail, old Gran hovers. Cocks her head. I try to hush a little sneeze, but . . .

"Hah!" says Gran, peering up. Then, humps her shoulders, thrashes in through the snowberry thicket. She doesn't know the path to my tree is only for hands and knees. I am an acorn. Tiny. Way high.

"Acorn, are you?"

"Climb up, Gran," say I. It's a fair catch.

"Too old," says Gran. She is puffing. "You do the climbing. I'll knit sunset." She settles down and hauls out her yarn. Tickety tick her needles say, chattering over a scarlet square.

"Ask me where I am, Gran."

"Where are you?"

"Castle keep," I say.

"Dungeon deep," says Gran. She has the key!

"Ask me again, Gran."

"Where are you now, honey bunch?"

"Avast, me hearty," I shout. The sea jumps up.
"Thar she blows," calls Gran.
"Find me now," I drawl.
"Where are you, baby doll?"
"The lone prairie!"
"Git along, little dogie," sings Gran.
The wind joins in, "Ty yi yo!"

"Look at your knees! Both of you!" Mom brushes us down on the back porch. Gran and I are horses. We snort for our hay. We eat by ourselves in the kitchen. All the better.

"You found me, Gran," I tell her.

"Finders keepers," says Gran. During dessert we practice whistling.

Day after day we hie to our tree. I climb, Gran knits,
tickety tick. She smoothes out a square, white flecks on
blue.

"I call this one 'Sparks on the Sea,'" she says.

"Sparks on the Sea!" I shout it loud so the sparks can
hear.

"And this one," she coos, waving a square striped
yellow and brown, "is 'Bee Song.'"

Gran knits everything. Pink and green for "Shooting
Star," gold for "Blossom on the Broom." "Chocolate lily"
is speckled brown. She knits them up and names them.

"Goodness, what was I thinking of?" says Gran,
fussing over a sandy square.

"Cricket's Chirp?" I am only guessing.

"Exactly!" crows Gran. "Aren't you my clever girl?"
When Gran knits, the world goes gleeful.

Spring, we rescue a robin flopped from its nest, a baby chick no bigger than my hand. Its neck is a thread. Its feathers aren't nearly enough. We give it seeds and a soft bed, but we cannot make it live.

"Back to the bosom," says Gran, tucking purple yarn all round. We bury it deep, safe from beasts, in a secret place where lilies nod their sleepy heads.

Summer, we bring snacks for chickadees. They sit on our hands, crazy for peanuts. We like treats, too, and sneak them from the kitchen. Snowberries plump out. Gran and I pop them on the trail. They hiss under our heels. Crickets sing, "Hot, hot." Broom pods rattle and snap. Gran's my old pal.

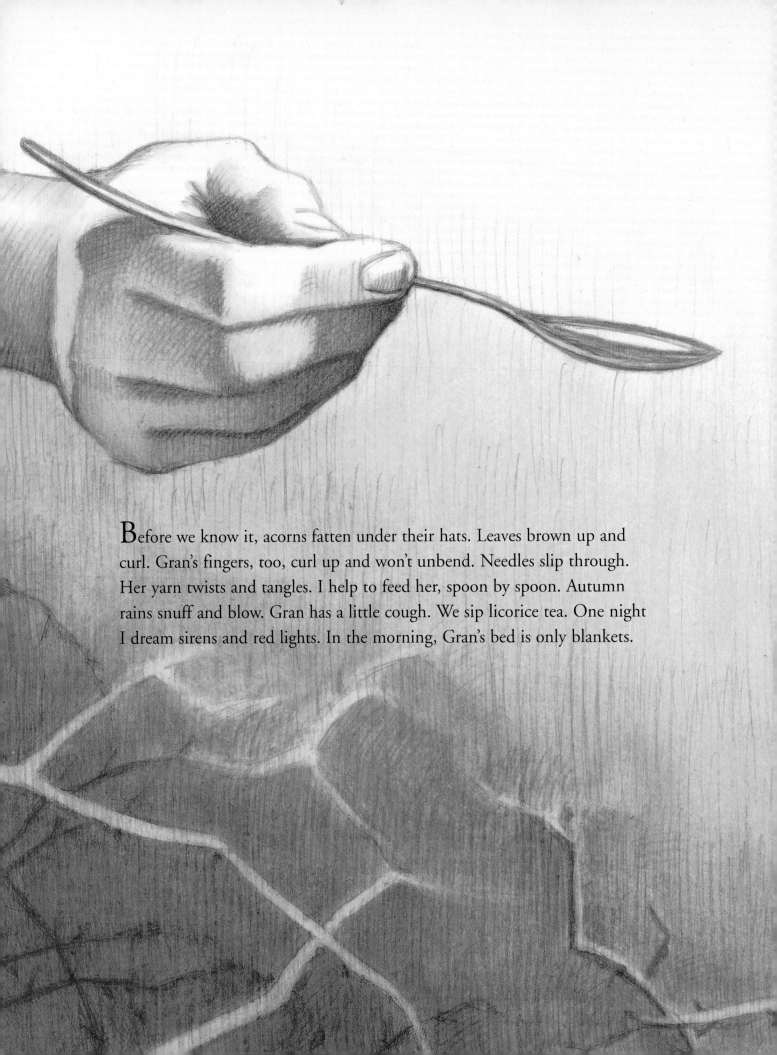

Before we know it, acorns fatten under their hats. Leaves brown up and curl. Gran's fingers, too, curl up and won't unbend. Needles slip through. Her yarn twists and tangles. I help to feed her, spoon by spoon. Autumn rains snuff and blow. Gran has a little cough. We sip licorice tea. One night I dream sirens and red lights. In the morning, Gran's bed is only blankets.

"Where's my gran?"
"Hospital."
"Why?"
"She's very ill."
"A sniffle," I cry. "A sniffle! I'll be her nurse. I have hankies."
"Oh, my dear," says Mom. Her arms offer a nest for me.

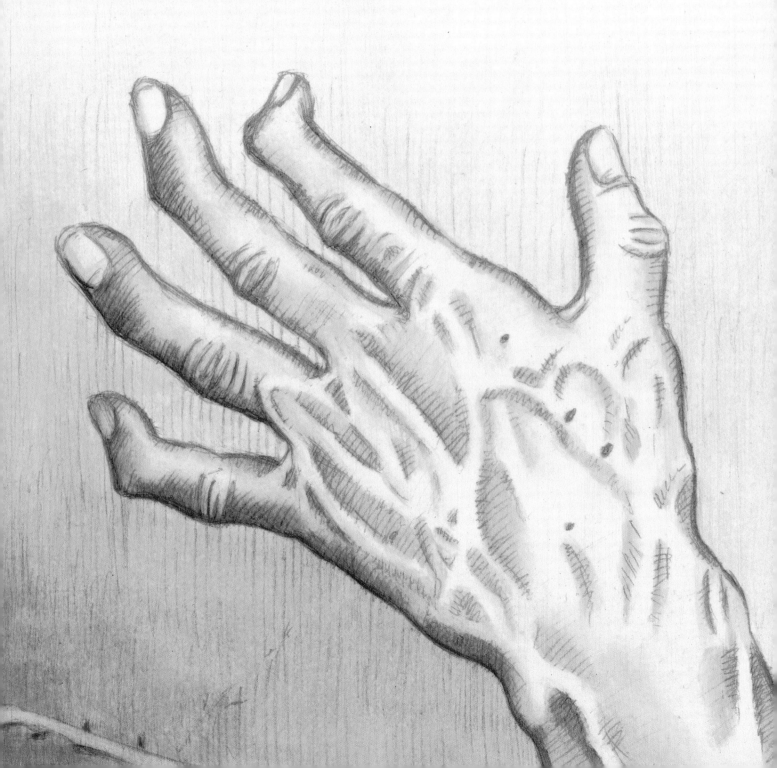

After school, I puff hard up that hospital hill. I whirl through the whirring doors and ding that desk bell until a face pops up.

"No children without parents," thin lips hiss. "See, it says so on the sign." Her finger points and taps.

What would you do if you were me? Would you duck past that sign and fly up the stairs to rescue your gran? Would you gather her wool and stand on guard while she knits up a ship and a sail? Would the two of you launch from the window and soar away, back to your stouthearted tree? Would your gran knit a stronghold high in the branches? Would you live there like wild girls on berries the birds bring?

Or would you do like me? Hang around outside on the hospital lawn and long for your gran to wave from a window, and when it got dark trudge home to Mom.

Mom is afraid to take me.

"Your gran is so changed."

Do I care? Would you?

Gran lies on pillows, very still. Bottles and tubes, bottles and tubes. Very quiet, old pal, Gran.

"Gran?" Her face is gray without the dandy makeup. "Gran! Ask me where I am." Bone and skin, bone and skin, hands all crooked on the coverlet. I slip my fingers in. "Gran, I'm in the castle keep. I'm up in the crow's nest, Gran." Her cheek is velvet to my lips. "I'll save you, Gran," I say, but I don't know how.

Winter oaks drip bare and black. Leafless branches knock elbows in the wind. Rain pelts, trail goes to mud. Gum boots slip and stick. Our tree is old and black and brittle. Gran is gone. Ashes to ashes.

"It's a blessing," says Mom. It's not a blessing to me.

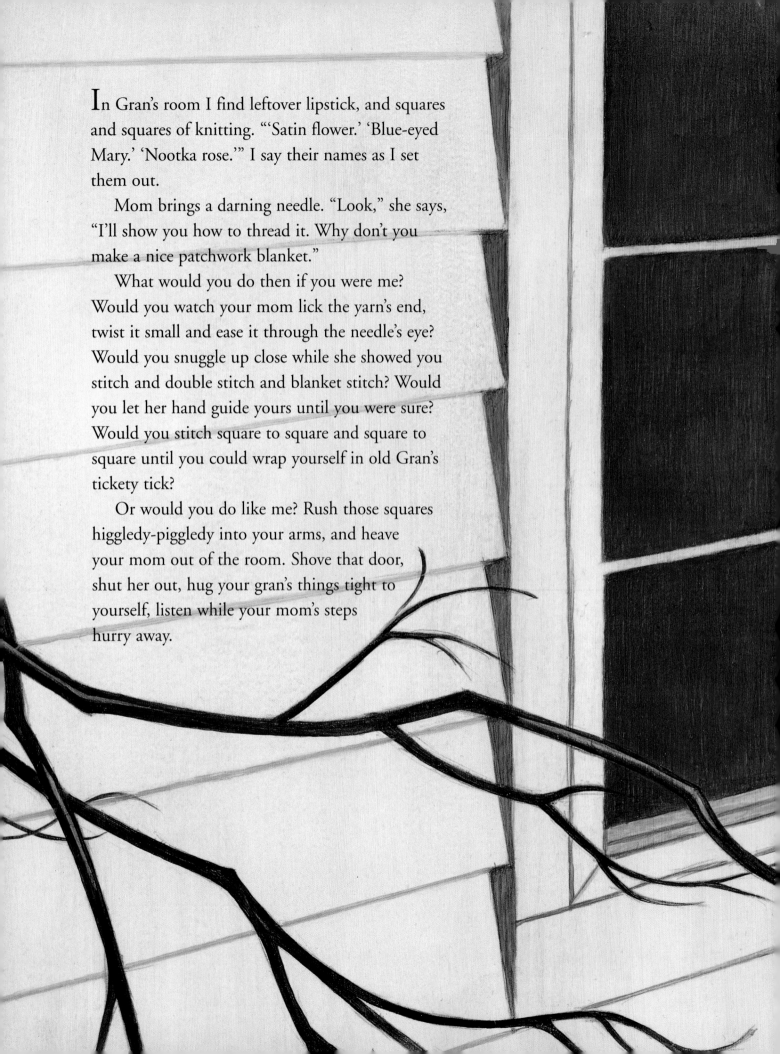

In Gran's room I find leftover lipstick, and squares and squares of knitting. "'Satin flower.' 'Blue-eyed Mary.' 'Nootka rose.'" I say their names as I set them out.

Mom brings a darning needle. "Look," she says, "I'll show you how to thread it. Why don't you make a nice patchwork blanket."

What would you do then if you were me? Would you watch your mom lick the yarn's end, twist it small and ease it through the needle's eye? Would you snuggle up close while she showed you stitch and double stitch and blanket stitch? Would you let her hand guide yours until you were sure? Would you stitch square to square and square to square until you could wrap yourself in old Gran's tickety tick?

Or would you do like me? Rush those squares higgledy-piggledy into your arms, and heave your mom out of the room. Shove that door, shut her out, hug your gran's things tight to yourself, listen while your mom's steps hurry away.

Spring comes anyhow, dries up mud, calls out quail babies. I see from my window the oak grove greening. Moss will be bright, I know where; shooting stars start up, I know where. Lilies will push through, I know that secret place. Where's my gran?

One day Mom says, "Come out to the woods. We'll scatter Gran's ashes." She has a white box.

"Gran's in there?" I know she's not, not Gran. Not lipstick, hot pink cheeks, not sunset yarns and green and gold in there. No, but what? My hand dips in. Grit and grain, gray and clean. We walk in step, my mom and me, sowing Gran's ashes along the trail. Arcs of them fly and fall. Rattle on leaf and sift through grass.

"When I was a little girl like you, and your gran was my mama . . ." Mom's stories come out, scraps and squares, higgledy-piggledy, out of her mouth. I never knew. She loved Gran, too. Tears well out of us and trickle down. Grins tickle up and bubble out. Gran would love this!

"Back to the bosom of the earth," says Mom. Her hand is gentle on my head.

"My tree is over there," I say.
"It's a beautiful tree," says Mom.

My tree stands stout. Its bark rasps a welcome as I boost up. Leaves burst out to catch the sun. I am up the crow's nest. "Land ho!" Canada flaps at the flagpole. Chickadees swoop and scold.

"Where's our treats?" Sea jumps up. Wind is velvet on my lips.

"See me now, Mom. See me, Gran!"

Northern Lights Books for Children are published by
Red Deer Press
56 Avenue & 32 Street Box 5005
Red Deer Alberta Canada T4N 5H5

Credits
Edited for the Press by Peter Carver
Cover and text design by Blair Kerrigan/Glyphics and Ron Lightburn
Printed in Hong Kong for Red Deer Press

Acknowledgments
Financial support provided by the Canada Council, the Department of Canadian Heritage and the Alberta Foundation for the Arts, a beneficiary of the Lottery Fund of the Government of Alberta.

COMMITTED TO THE DEVELOPMENT OF CULTURE AND THE ARTS

The illustrations for this book started out as black and white pencil drawings on 8 1/2" x 11" bond paper. Photocopies of these drawings were coated with a clear acrylic medium and then colored with oil paints.

Canadian Cataloguing in Publication Data
Gregory, Nan.
Wild Girl and Gran
(Northern lights books for children)
ISBN 0-88995-221-3
1. Lightburn, Ron. II. Title. III. Series.
PS8563.R4438W54 2000   jC813'.54   C00-910480-1
PZ7.G86235Wi 2000

5 4 3 2 1

For Sol, who loved his gran.
– Nan Gregory

To teachers and librarians everywhere, for sharing their love of books.
With thanks to Trissa and Susan for bringing Wild Girl to life.
– Ron Lightburn

Wild Girl's tree is a Garry oak. It grows in a very rare, very beautiful ecosystem known as a Garry oak meadow. In Canada these meadows are found only in the southwest corner of British Columbia. There are over one thousand species of plants and animals in Garry oak meadows. The native plants mentioned in the story are

Garry oak – *Quercus garryana*

Snowberry – *Symphoricarpos albus*

Shooting star – *Dodecatheon hendersonii*

Chocolate lily – *Fritillaria lanceolata*

White fawn lily – *Erythronium oregonum*

Satin flower – *Sisyrinchium douglasii*

Blue-eyed Mary – *Collinsia grandiflora*

Nootka rose – *Rosa nutkana*

There is also an eager stranger from Scotland:

Scotch broom – *Cytisus scoparius*